Guardian

Also by Julius Lester

Let's Talk About Race

Pharaoh's Daughter

Guardian

Julius Lester

Amistad

HARPER TEEN

An Imprint of HarperCollins*Publishers*

Amistad and HarperTeen are imprints of HarperCollins Publishers.

Guardian
Copyright © 2008 by Julius Lester
All rights reserved. Printed in the United States of America.
No part of this book may be used or reproduced in any manner whatsoever
without written permission except in the case of brief quotations
embodied in critical articles and reviews. For information address
HarperCollins Children's Books, a division of HarperCollins Publishers,
1350 Avenue of the Americas, New York, NY 10019.
www.harperteen.com

Library of Congress Cataloging-in-Publication Data
Lester, Julius.
Guardian / by Julius Lester. — 1st ed.
p. cm.
Summary: In a rural southern town in 1946, a white man and his son watch the
lynching of an innocent black man. Includes historical note on lynching.
Includes bibliographical references (p.   ).
ISBN 978-0-06-155890-0 (trade bdg.) — ISBN 978-0-06-155891-7 (lib.)
[1. Lynching–Fiction. 2. Racism–Fiction. 3. Race relations–Fiction. 4. African
Americans–Fiction. 5. Southern States–History–1865-1951–Fiction.] I. Title.
PZ7.L5629Gu 2008   2008014251
[Fic]–dc22   CIP
                                                         AC

Typography by Alison Klapthor
1   2   3   4   5   6   7   8   9   10
❖
First Edition

In memory of the more than four thousand men and women, black and white, who were victims of lynchings, and those we will never know.

— J.L.

Trees remember.

They talk among themselves about "the winter of sixty-two when the snow was so heavy it broke limbs on the Father oak tree in the church cemetery. We were worried he might not survive."

"And what about the summer it hardly rained and we had to send our roots deep into the earth to find water?" they reminisce.

But some trees do not speak, not even to the birds that find delicious insects hidden beneath their bark, not even to the birds building nests on their branches thick with leaves. These are the old trees whose ponderous, arching branches create cool shade.

They do not speak because they are ashamed.

At least ones in the South are.

They were used for evil. Even though they could

not defend themselves, they are still ashamed.

Sometimes when the wind caresses their leaves, they whisper to the breezes, telling them what they have seen and heard, telling those invisible messengers how they were used as accomplices in evil.

The wind can listen for only so long to such painful memories. To rid itself of the horror threaded into the bark and rings of the trees, the wind goes high into the sky where it can expel the suffering of the trees without hurting anything or anyone.

But there are times when a tree can no longer withstand the pain inflicted on it, and the wind will take pity on that tree and topple it over in a mighty storm. All the other trees who witnessed the evil look down upon the fallen tree with envy. They pray for the day when a wind will end their suffering.

I pray for the day when God will end mine.

Tuesday—Midafternoon

Summer 1946.

Davis, a small town in the deep South of the United States.

Fourteen-year-old Ansel Anderson stands by the screen door in the entrance of the store his grandfather started, the store where Ansel's father worked beside his father when he was a boy, the store where Ansel now works beside his father.

It is late afternoon. The heat is as heavy as a broken heart.

Nothing moves, not the leaves on the large oak tree at the end of the concrete island in the middle of the main street, not the three men sitting on a bench in the tree's shade, not even a bird.

On the other side of the street, the clothing,

shoe, and drug stores are as empty of customers as Anderson's.

Long before Ansel was born, when his grandfather ran Anderson's General Store, they carried clothes, shoes, and remedies in addition to the groceries, rifles, ammunition, and fishing equipment they carried now. Bert, Ansel's father, took over the store after his father dropped dead behind the counter from a heart attack because, Bert believed, the store had tried to be everything to everybody. That was a good way to give yourself a heart attack, not run a business. Bert was only eighteen when his father died, but he consolidated the inventory and increased profitability.

Ansel has worked in the store since he can remember. One day it will be his. He is not sure he will be as good at it as his father is.

Bert is a congenial and handsome man with curly, dark hair, blue eyes, and a smile that could steal honey from bees.

Many people, especially women, come to the store as much for his smile as to buy what they need. Bert knows people need a smile as much as they need to buy milk.

People almost always leave the store feeling better than when they came in, and all because Bert smiled at them.

Ansel is more like his mother—short, dark straight hair, dark eyes. She looks younger than her thirty-two years, and he certainly looks younger than his fourteen.

His mother, Maureen, used to work in the store every day after she and Bert married six months before Ansel was born. But she only works Saturdays now. That's when Zeph Davis, or Cap'n Davis, as everyone, white and colored, calls him, brings his Negroes into town.

They don't have money. They work on shares. He takes care of all their needs—a shack to live in, clothes to wear, food to eat, cottonseed, and everything else they might need. In the fall when they pick the cotton and bring it to Cap'n Davis to be weighed, he deducts their expenses from what he would have paid them for the cotton, and their expenses include the cheese and crackers and sodas they buy at Anderson's every Saturday. Their expenses are always greater than what Cap'n Davis pays them for the cotton they grow, so each year they end up deeper in debt to him than they were the year before. It is another form of slavery.

Ansel's mother is the one who writes in the big ledger book what the Negroes buy and how much it costs.

There is a dour seriousness about her and Ansel. Both mother and son are cloaked in melancholy, a sadness arising, perhaps, from the land in which the sorrowing trees spread their roots, a despair that their lives have as little meaning as the dust stirred up by a passing car.

It worries Bert that Ansel is so much like his mother. The boy can't seem to grasp a simple thing like how important it is to smile at customers. "People buy as much because they like you as because they need something."

"What if I don't feel like smiling?" Ansel asked his father once.

Bert had gotten angry. "There ain't no place for feelings in business. Your job is to see to it that people who come in for one thing leave with two, three, or four. The only thing you should be feeling is how you can get somebody to believe he needs something, whether he does or not. People don't want to feel like

6

you're taking their money. Smile, and they'll feel like they're giving it to you."

"But that's not honest," Ansel had insisted.

Bert smiled. "It is if you're running a business!"

Ansel turns away from the door and goes over to his father, who is seated behind the counter.

"Papa? Do you need me and Willie for anything?"

Bert looks at his son. He remembers what it was like when he was fourteen and stood looking out the screen door on a day like today thinking he was going to die of boredom. He would not have minded closing the store and going home, but if he did, as sure as he was breathing, somebody would come to town wanting something.

"I reckon not. You and Willie going to do a little fishing?"

"Yes, sir."

"Y'all can go on. But tomorrow's Wednesday. You and Willie have to take groceries and supplies out to Miz Esther's first thing."

"Yes, sir. Thanks, Papa." Ansel runs eagerly to the storage room at the back of the store where Willie is.

Bert frowns as he hears the two excited voices.

He had hired Willie for the summer because Esther Davis had asked him to. As far as Bert was concerned, a nigger boy like that ought to be out working in the field, but his mama was Esther's cook and housekeeper, and his father was crazy. There wasn't anybody he could work in the fields with.

Bert didn't need the boy, but he couldn't refuse to do something a Davis asked, even one as eccentric as Esther.

He had to admit that the boy worked hard keeping the storage room neat and organized, shelving goods, and packing groceries. Him doing what Ansel would normally be doing had given Bert the opportunity to start teaching his son the business—how to do the ordering, from whom and for what, how to keep track of inventory, and how to total up the receipts at the end of each day.

But if Bert had known Ansel and the nigger would take to each other like the brother neither one of them had, he would not have hired him. He kept looking for an excuse to fire him, but the boy never gave him one.

It was all right to have a nigger as a friend when

you were little, but at fourteen it was time for Ansel to understand what it meant to be white, and past time for Willie to understand what it meant to be a nigger. Next summer there wouldn't be any work at the store for Willie, no matter how much Esther begged him.

Bert walks from behind the counter and goes to stand in the doorway where Ansel had been. He stares idly at the statue of the Confederate soldier at the head of the concrete island, his rifle pointed at anyone coming into town. He doesn't have to see the base to remember the words carved there: "To our Confederate Army dead who struggled valiantly to preserve our way of life."

They might have lost the war, but their way of life hadn't really changed, at least not in Davis. A nigger didn't speak until spoken to; he looked down at his feet when talking to a white person—man, woman, or child; he stepped off the sidewalk and walked in the street when he saw a white person coming toward him or heard one behind him; and he'd better not even look like he was *thinking* about being equal to a white man.

Maureen didn't like him referring to them as niggers. He didn't call them that to their faces, unlike every other white person in town. But he didn't address them as "Mister" or "Miz," either. He addressed them by name. He'd learned that from his father.

But also like his father, when Bert was around other whites, at church or wherever, he said "nigger." Everybody would have looked at him suspiciously if he referred to them as "colored" or "Negro." Hell, even Reverend Dennis called them "niggers," and if the preacher did it, there wasn't nothing wrong with it.

Recently Maureen had been talking about how she wondered if Davis was a good place to raise a boy, if Ansel might get a better education in a school up north.

She had to know that he would never let Ansel leave Davis, but if he did, it wouldn't be to go up north where niggers thought they were as good as white people.

Deep down, Bert knows different, but that doesn't mean he could give up the good feeling it gave him to be a white man.

It was a feeling he had somehow failed to pass

on to his son. The boy was too close to his mother. That was the problem.

Bert knew he had to do something before the boy grew up to be unfit to live in a place like Davis, unfit to be a member of the white race.

Tuesday—Late Afternoon

1.

At the back of the store is an area of gravel where delivery trucks come. Beyond this is a large field overgrown with weeds, wildflowers, and Queen Anne's lace. A hobbled mule grazes idly.

Ansel and Willie make their way along the path through the field, Willie carrying a fishing pole in each hand, Ansel carrying a can of worms. The path continues through a small stand of tulip poplar trees and emerges in a clearing at the bank of a wide creek of clear water.

"Look at that one!" Ansel exclaims, pointing to a huge catfish on the bottom, swishing its tail languidly. The two boys sit down on the bank, bait their hooks, and throw the lines into the water.

For a while neither says a word. There is something special about the silence this afternoon. It isn't the first time the two have gone fishing together here. But this afternoon it is as if they are outside time, free of the definitions that constrict their lives inside time. On this afternoon they are merely two boys doing what boys have always done when it is summer and there's a creek nearby and fish lolling on the bottom.

Ansel is the one who finally breaks the silence, but not because the silence is too much to bear. It is the intimate quality of the silence that encourages him to speak.

"I saw your papa Friday evening."

Big Willie. That's the only name Ansel knows for him, but he doesn't use it. He knows it is all right for him to call colored people by their first names. Indeed, it is expected of him. But Willie can't call Ansel's father "Bert"; Ansel doesn't think he should call Willie's father "Big Willie."

Ansel also doesn't think Willie should address him as "Mister Ansel," especially when they are by themselves.

But no matter how many times Ansel has asked Willie to call him "Ansel," all Willie says is "Can't."

Ansel is ashamed to admit that a part of him likes it when Willie calls him "Mister Ansel." It makes him feel important.

"Me and my papa had just closed up the store," Ansel continues quietly, "and were walking to our car, which was parked next to the church. We saw your papa coming out the back door of the church. Does he like working there?"

Little Willie's mother and father think Bert Anderson is the best white man in the world, because Big Willie was shell-shocked when he came back from the war over in Germany and wasn't fit to do much of anything.

Esther Davis knew the church needed a new roof, and she asked Bert to speak with Reverend Dennis and tell him that she would pay for the roof if he hired Big Willie to do little jobs around the church—clean up, set out chairs in the social hall for meetings, and be the general handyman. And she would pay Willie's salary, but he was to think it came from the church.

"He likes it real good," Little Willie responds. "He say when he's in the church, he don't see things."

"What kind of things?" Ansel wants to know. He knew Big Willie wasn't quite right in the head because

14

he wandered around talking to himself, sometimes very loudly.

"Almost every night my papa wakes up yelling about mountains made of bodies, and about skeletons walking around, except he say the skeletons were live people."

"He does?" Ansel asks, trying to imagine a mountain made of bodies and can't.

Little Willie nods. "Once I said to my mama that Papa didn't make sense when he say things like that. I told her that mountains are made of rocks, not bodies, and skeletons couldn't walk around like people."

"What did your mama say?"

"She say, 'Just because something don't make no sense, it don't mean it didn't happen.'"

Ansel is on the verge of saying something, something important, when he hears a boy and a girl laughing, coming toward them.

With a pain that will remain in his heart for the rest of his long life, Ansel recognizes the girl's laughter immediately. It is a laugh that rings with the joy of bells in church at Christmastime, a laugh he thought only he was supposed to hear.

He also recognizes the high-pitched and tight

laugh of the boy that sounds like he is in a lacerating pain.

That laugh thrusts Willie and Ansel brutally back into time.

Without a word or a glance at Ansel, Willie jerks his line from the water and starts wrapping it around the pole.

Ansel does not know what to do. He does not want to turn around and look at them, at her. But he can't help himself. Maybe he is wrong. Maybe it is not her.

He turns just as the two emerge from the trees, just in time to see Zeph Davis III put his arm around her shoulders like she is a big teddy bear he won playing a game at the carnival.

When Mary Susan sees Ansel looking up at her, her face flushes red. She tries to move away from Zeph's arm, but he, eyebrows raised in recognition at Ansel, pulls her to him tightly, his fingers digging into her shoulder.

Zeph saunters down to the creek bank, down to where Little Willie and Ansel sit.

The sun is behind Mary. The way the light glistens off her blond hair, it looks to Ansel like she has a halo around her head like the angels in the stained-glass windows of her father's church.

Mary Susan is looking down at the ground.

Ansel continues staring at her. She is tall, taller than he is, as tall as Zeph. With her blond hair and blue eyes, she is the most beautiful girl in town, if not the entire county, and if someone said she was the most beautiful girl in the state, and even the South, Ansel would not have argued.

She radiates the purity of innocence, a look she practices before the mirror in her room. She isn't sure how she does it, or even why, but she has learned to make her eyes wide, as if she lives in a perpetual childhood where there are no skinned knees or tears, or fathers putting their hands where they do not belong.

This summer, almost overnight it seems, her body, through no effort on her part, has unfolded, like bee-kissed flowers, into its woman-shape, and before she can learn how to live with the monthly streaming of blood and the weight of breasts, she is the target of male lust—adolescent, adult, and aged. Even at church, when she walks down the aisle to the altar to take communion, she feels male eyes moving up and down her body like spiders across a web. She does not understand how her father can preach against lust and make her feel as if she has no clothes on. She knows those eyes want something of her, from her, and she is flattered and repulsed at the same time. If only she had someone to talk to who could help her figure out what to do, help her figure out how to be.

No one in Davis is aware enough to articulate that almost no male could resist the compelling blending of her new, thrusting breasts with the innocence in her blue eyes, an innocence which belies knowledge of anything as carnal as nipples hardening with flushed excitement, a purity unsullied by the pungent odors that accompany the blush of womanhood that causes male eyes to flame with a desire that can never be satisfied. She was child and woman, an especially vulnerable time in the life of one as beautiful as she.

At this moment, she feels Ansel's eyes looking at her from a depth of pain she did not know could exist, and she is sorry she allowed her summertime boredom to lead her to agree to taking a walk with Zeph.

When she asked her father if it was all right for her to go with Zeph, she had thought, had hoped he would say no. She saw the "no" in his eyes and how quickly it was replaced by fear, but not a fear for her. It was the fear of what might happen if he said no to a Davis. The church depended on the generosity of the Davises.

Mary Susan was surprised by the contempt she felt for her father at that moment when she needed him to protect her from herself. Instead, he was asking her to protect him.

Then she walked out of the trees and saw Ansel. When her family had moved to town last summer, he had been the only boy whose look gave her to herself, whose look did not make her feel like eyes were unbuttoning her blouse and pulling down her skirt.

"Well, well, well," Zeph says, looking down at Ansel and Willie. "If it ain't the nigger lover with his tar baby."

Zeph Davis is sixteen, the great-grandson of the Zephaniah Davis who gave his name to the town, the son of Cap'n Davis, who owns the largest plantation in that part of the state, as well as every building in the center of town, including Anderson's General Store.

Willie has finished wrapping his line around the

pole and securing the hook. He gets up and walks away without looking at anyone.

Ansel does not want him to go, does not want to be left alone with Zeph, does not want to be left alone with Zeph and Mary. But he, too, pulls his line from the water.

"Where you goin', Tar Baby?" Zeph calls after Willie.

Willie knows he cannot walk away when a white person speaks to him. He stops and turns. He is careful not to look Zeph in the eyes, careful not to look at Mary Susan at all, and focuses his gaze on a spot in front of Zeph's boots.

"I don't want no trouble, Mister Zeph, suh. Don't want no trouble."

Zeph laughs. "You a good nigger, boy. You can go on."

"Thank you, suh," and Willie turns and runs into the stand of trees.

Zeph laughs his high-pitched, strangled laugh, then makes an exaggerated motion of sniffing the air. "Smells better already. I know niggers wash with soap, but can't nothing get rid of that nigger smell, can it, Mary?"

Ansel has finished fixing his line and hook to his pole. He stands up and looks at Mary Susan.

"Where you going, nigger lover?" Zeph asks.

Ansel is glad when Mary Susan says, "Don't call him that."

"But that's what he is! What's wrong with calling him by his right name? And why do you care? I know you and him are sweet on each other, but nobody but another nigger lover would be sweet on a nigger lover. And I know you're not one of them. Are you?" There is a menacing tone to his voice.

Ansel's eyes plead with Mary Susan to say something, but she won't look at him.

Zeph pulls her closer and gives her a hard, clumsy kiss on the lips.

Tears come into Ansel's eyes, and afraid Zeph and Mary Susan will see, he runs into the trees.

Zeph's shrieking laugh follows him.

2.

Willie is sitting on the ground, his back against the store, his thin arms crossed tightly against his chest, his fishing pole leaning against the doorjamb.

Ansel takes the poles and the can of worms he remembered to bring and puts them just inside the back door. Then he sits down next to Willie.

They are silent, but this silence is that of an anger that knows its name but dares not speak. But Willie must speak, or the anger will claim him, body, soul, and mind.

"Zeph Davis" is all Willie says.

"You know him?"

"Know that noise he calls laughing."

"Where you know him from?"

"He come out to the quarters all the time. He have a pistol jammed in his belt. One time he shoot Cousin Dan's coon dog that was sleeping in the yard just because he could."

"Why did he do that?"

Willie looks at Ansel, eyes contemptuous with knowledge. "Why you think? If he see a nigger girl he wants, he just takes her. He'll take her into the cabin where she live at, and make her mama and papa watch while he has his way with her. When he come out, he be laughing, but my mama say it sound to her like he be crying."

Ansel looks toward the creek, wondering if Zeph is having his way with Mary Susan.

3.

As Ansel walks away, Mary Susan wants to call out to him to wait, that she is sorry, that she does not know why she is standing there letting Zeph Davis put his arm around her as if she is his property.

Perhaps she would have said something, have done something if Zeph had not jerked her head around and started pressing his lips against hers. She is so surprised that for a moment she does not know what is happening.

When she does, she tries to pull away from him, but he puts one hand behind her head and pushes her lips even harder against his.

This is not how she imagined her first kiss, and certainly she had never dreamed it would be from Zeph Davis. Her first kiss was supposed to have come from Ansel, and it would have been soft and gentle and kind.

Suddenly, she feels Zeph's tongue poking at her closed mouth and does not know what he is trying to do until his tongue is inside her mouth, and she can taste his day—the sausage he had for breakfast, the cigarettes he smoked, the mouthwash he gargled to cover the smell, the dust that billowed up from the road and into the truck he drove around his father's plantation. She does not want the knowledge of him in her mouth, and she bites his tongue as hard as she can.

"Bitch! You goddam bitch!" Zeph yells, involuntarily releasing his grip on her.

He tries to slap her, but some instinct causes Mary Susan to move away from his avenging hand.

"You try to hit me one more time, and I'll kick you so hard in a certain place you won't be able to get out of bed for a month."

Fear comes into Zeph's eyes.

"Just because I'm the preacher's daughter, it don't mean that I don't know things."

"You goddam bitch!" Zeph snarls again, but his voice is tinged with wariness.

The two stare at each other for a moment, he waiting for her to leave first so he can feel like he won, she waiting for him to leave first because she is afraid to turn her back on him.

Finally, he flings another "goddam bitch" at her and walks away.

Mary Susan waits until she is sure he is gone,

then tears of anger and fear, of disgust and confusion fill her eyes and trickle slowly down her face. She sits down at the edge of the creek, sits down where she thinks Ansel was sitting.

She does not understand what she'd been thinking by going with Zeph. She doesn't even like him.

But she was flattered that an older boy, the son of the richest man in town, would be interested in her.

He was taller than she was, and she didn't have to look down at him like she did Ansel. He also wore regular clothes—a shirt, pants, and shoes.

Zeph reminded her of the boys in Atlanta, where her father had had a big church, not a little country church like this one. But something had happened. She didn't know what, but the next thing she knew they were living here where the most exciting thing to happen was a bird shitting on the statue in the square.

She liked Ansel, but seeing him in his overalls and no shirt nor shoes, he was everything she hated about Davis.

What was wrong with wanting a little excitement, something to break the monotony of one hot day after another, something to disrupt the enervating boredom of seeing the same faces day after day after day?

She sighs deeply. What has she done? Why wasn't life like a blackboard that you could write on, and if you made a mistake, you could take an eraser, wipe the mistake away, and start over?

What was going to happen now? How could she ever look at Ansel again? And Zeph.

She doesn't know what she is more afraid of now, Ansel's hurt or Zeph's anger.

Mary Susan wipes the tears from her face, gets up, and walks slowly through the trees and across the field to the back of the store.

Ansel isn't there.

4.

"Crazy bitch!" Zeph mutters to himself, tasting blood in his mouth as he comes out of the trees. He sees Ansel and the nigger boy sitting behind the store. But when they see him, they get up and hurry inside.

Zeph smiles and chuckles to himself.

He moves his tongue gingerly against the backs of his teeth. It still hurts but not as bad. Zeph continues along the dirt road at the back of the store until he comes to the street.

On the other side is the cemetery. Next to it is the church where Mary Susan's father is the preacher, then the parsonage.

Zeph had thought she would be sitting on the porch with nothing to do. That's why he walked by.

She was certainly very pretty, but he didn't know if he would have wanted her if she hadn't been the preacher's daughter. Well, that and them new titties of hers sticking out like an invitation to a party.

Wouldn't it be something if he got a piece of that!

Just thinking about it made Zeph grin.

Then he remembered what she said she would do

to him, and his lips return to their customary position of barely suppressed rage.

"Goddam bitch!" he mutters again. If he says it enough times, maybe the words will eradicate his humiliation, but he only gets more angry.

He is afraid she will tell Annie Forest, her best friend, and Annie Forest couldn't keep a secret if her life depended on it, and before he knows it, everybody in town will know.

Instead of turning right and going to the center of town, he turns in the opposite direction. A short distance beyond the church he comes to a little bridge that goes over the same creek where Ansel and Willie had been fishing.

Instead of crossing the bridge, Zeph slides down the embankment and walks under it. He takes a pocketknife from his pocket. Then he squats and waits.

He is silent and still except for the fingers of his right hand, which idly caress the folded knife.

He doesn't have to wait long before he sees what he is waiting for.

For someone else, the frog would have been hard to see against the dirt and in the deep shadows beneath the bridge. But not for Zeph. He has been doing this as long as he can remember.

The frog hops. Then stops. It waits. Detecting no movement, it hops again. Then stops. Waits.

Like a snake, Zeph does not even blink. His fingers cease their idle stroking of the knife. He watches the frog hop closer and closer to him.

The frog is next to his right shoe, but Zeph waits. The frog waits.

The frog's next hop brings it to the space between Zeph's right and left shoes, and with a sudden swiftness that would have surprised everyone who knew him, he grabs the frog just as it is preparing to spring, having not sensed danger.

Zeph holds it so that its legs frantically move back and forth, try to leap but have nothing to push against except air.

While still holding the frog firmly in his left hand, Zeph puts the fingernail of his right thumb into the notch at the end of the knife's blade and flips it open.

He keeps the blade of his knife as sharp as hatred. You never know when you might come upon a snake, a baby bird, a kitten, or a frog.

He puts the frog on the ground, pressing hard

against its back, forcing its legs to splay outward.

With surgical precision he slices off one of the frog's hind legs, then takes away the hand that is holding it down.

Frantically, the frog moves its remaining leg back and forth, back and forth, trying to take a giant leap from a cruelty it did not know existed. Unable to leap, it nonetheless goes through its instinctive kicking motions, but to no avail.

Zeph Davis watches the frog intently, fascinated by the creature's spastic motions, by its desperate efforts to assert the life that is bleeding away.

As he watches the frog, anger starts leaving his body like the blood leaving the frog's.

He doesn't understand why, but any time an anger overtakes him, he has only to use his knife on a creature, and the anger seeps out.

It has been like that since he was little.

Not too many more moments pass before a cold calmness descends on him. The anger is gone.

Without emotion he plunges the knife into the frog's back, pinning it to the ground. The creature shudders and then is still.

Holding the frog to the ground with a finger of his

left hand, Zeph slowly pulls the knife from its body with his right. He goes to the creek and washes the blade in the cold water, then dries it with a few quick swipes on his jeans.

He returns to the now still body of the frog and stares down at it. Already ants are starting to swarm over the carcass.

"Don't forget to say grace."

He lets out a long slow breath and walks away. He feels better than even after he pleasures himself.

Tuesday Night

No emotion eats at your soul like shame, that feeling of having violated yourself, of having done something so wrong you can't imagine how to go on living.

Ansel lay in bed that night unable to sleep. It was as hot inside as it was out. He could smell the smudge pots his father had put on the front and back porches in a vain attempt to keep the mosquitoes out of the house.

Neither the heat nor the mosquitoes bother him as much as the memory of Zeph's arm around Mary Susan, as his lips on hers.

Over and over Ansel asks himself: Why didn't I ask Mary Susan what she was doing with a piece of trash like Zeph? His father might own everything and everybody in town, but his son was a piece of trash.

Ansel does not understand why he had not gone to Mary Susan, taken her hand, and led her away.

But what if she wouldn't have let him? What if she had said she wanted to be with Zeph?

Ansel didn't know what he would have done.

He didn't know anything about girls, and especially a girl from someplace big like Atlanta. Other boys were intimidated around her because she was the preacher's daughter. Ansel was scared of her because she was from the big city. What could she possibly see in a short country boy like him?

Whereas Zeph was older, taller, and he had gone places with his father—Nashville, New Orleans, even Atlanta.

Ansel knows what would have happened if Mary Susan had refused to walk away with him. He would have cried.

Zeph and Mary Susan would have laughed at him and told everyone in town that he was a crybaby.

But lying there in the darkness he realized that the humiliation of her rejecting him would not have been as great as the shame he began living with that night.

He was to learn that shame is an emotion that takes up residence in your heart, and its pain does not diminish with time. It only intensifies with each passing year.

Wednesday Morning

1.

Ansel is at the back of the store, filling the wagon with bags of groceries and canned goods. Willie brings the mule over from the field and hitches it to the wagon. They do not speak.

The two are almost finished loading the wagon when Ansel hears a voice from inside the store, hears a voice saying his name, a girl's voice, the voice he knows as well as his own.

He wants to see her, and yet, he never wants to see her again.

"Let's go, Willie," he says desperately, hurrying toward the wagon seat.

"Ain't that her coming?" Willie asks.

"I don't care. Let's go!"

But he does care. That's why he doesn't want to see her.

"Ansel?" Mary Susan's voice is soft, hesitant, trembling.

Ansel turns and looks at her. She is wearing an orange sundress and, to him, she is more beautiful than he ever dreamed a girl could be. But then he sees Zeph's arm around her, and he remembers the times he tried to put his arm around her and she moved away from his touch, saying, "What kind of girl do you think I am?"

"What do you want?" he asks, his voice harsh with hurt.

"About yesterday," she begins timidly.

"What about it?"

"It wasn't what it seemed like. I didn't know he was going to do that, put his arm around me. He did it just when he saw you through the trees. I felt bad about all the things he said."

"What are you doing being around somebody like that?" Ansel asks angrily.

"Like what? Zeph puts on this act to shock people. He likes to pretend he's bad, but he's not."

She knows what she is saying is not true, knows

she should not be defending Zeph, but Ansel's anger at her combined with her own anger at herself is about to annihilate her sense of her essential goodness, and she is frightened.

"You talk like you just lost your mind. All Zeph wants from you is one thing!"

"And what's that, Mr. Know-It-All?"

"You know. I don't need to say it. Can't you hear how Zeph would brag to everybody about what he did with the preacher's daughter?"

"Your mind is nasty! I wouldn't let him do that to me!"

"I didn't see you move away from him like you do me when I try to put my arm around you. I didn't see you saying no when he kissed you."

Tears spring to Mary Susan's eyes. She wants to tell Ansel how humiliated she felt with Zeph's arms around her, how she had bit him, how she had gone home and rinsed her mouth out.

She wants to tell him how much she hated Zeph touching her, how much she wants Ansel to forgive her. But Ansel is looking at her with such anger, with such hatred.

If she tells him she is afraid, he will let her feelings

drop into the dust at his feet or swat them away as if they were mosquitoes.

So she lashes out, wanting to hurt Ansel as much as he is hurting her.

"At least Zeph knows how to have fun and make a girl laugh. You're always so serious, Ansel. I get depressed just thinking about you."

Ansel turns away. "Let's go, Willie."

Mary Susan watches Ansel climb up to the seat, Willie following reluctantly. She knows she should not have said what she just did, but she doesn't know how to make the words go away.

Willie climbs up and takes the reins, pops them against the mule's rump, and the wagon starts to move.

"Ansel! I'm sorry!" Mary Susan calls out. "I didn't mean what I said. I'm sorry!"

Ansel hears her. He wants to tell Willie to stop the wagon.

"Don't you hear Miss Mary calling you?" Willie asks.

"Mind your own damn business, nig . . . ," and he stops.

Willie knows what Ansel was going to call him.

He is hurt. He knew better than to let himself start to trust.

Neither boy is old enough to understand that Ansel's stopping himself from uttering the word is more important than the fact that he almost said it.

2.

Esther Davis is a tall, thin, and not very attractive woman, a fact she has no illusions about. Her hair is a dull brown that she put into a bun when she was sixteen and hasn't changed since. Her nose is long and sharp, and her lips are so thin that if a male had ever tried to kiss her, he would not have known where.

She lives in the large house her father built on the town side of the railroad tracks, the house in which she was born.

Her parents sent her to prep school in Massachusetts when she was twelve, and neither they nor she had expected or wanted her to come back. An ugly girl with a sharp mind might have a better chance of finding a career for herself up north. As for a husband, well, no man wanted an ugly wife, especially if she was smarter than he was.

But her father had a stroke the year after she finished Radcliffe and had started teaching French at Boston Latin. Her mother needed her to help care for him.

The stroke had left him paralyzed and unable to speak, which she took as God's punishment of a man who treated his hunting dogs better than the Negroes whose work had made his father and him wealthy. Given a choice between shooting a deer or a Negro, her father would have been hard-pressed to choose.

She had thought she would stay a year. But near the end of that year, her mother died.

It took him ten miserable years to die, also a sign of God's punishment, but it became hers, too. She had been away from teaching too long. And the colored children on the plantation needed her.

Her brother, Zeph Jr., the new "Cap'n Davis," didn't want her teaching "my niggers how to write and do figures." He wanted her out of Davis.

But her father's will left her the house and money enough to live comfortably the rest of her life.

So she stayed to do penance for the deeds of her father, brother, and nephew.

Of the three, Zeph the Third was the worst, and that was saying a lot. She went to the cabins after his "visits," bringing cotton and salve to help tend the girl he had violated.

She hated her brother and nephew, not only because they were evil but also because their evil was nonchalant and devoid of passion. A cold evil was a frightening thing.

She did what she could, taking care of the old ones who couldn't tend cotton anymore. The groceries and supplies from Anderson's each week were almost exclusively for the Negroes.

But it was past time for her to go back where she belonged. She missed walking around Harvard Square with her choice of bookstores to enter, missed being able to see the latest movies, go to restaurants, or even something as simple as turning on the radio and being able to find classical music.

But there was one thing she had to do before she left. If she succeeded, she would not go back alone.

3.

Willie pulls the wagon up to the back of the Davis mansion. The back door opens and a young black woman comes out. She is as pretty as Esther Davis is ugly. This is Amanda, Willie's mother.

After helping Willie and Ansel unload the wagon, she asks the boys, "Do you have to hurry back to the store?"

"No, ma'am," Ansel answers. He knows that he isn't supposed to say "ma'am" to a colored lady, but this is Willie's mother. Willie says "ma'am" to Ansel's mother. Why shouldn't he say "ma'am" to Willie's?

"Miz Davis would like to talk to the two of you."

Ansel and Willie exchange worried glances. What could she want to talk to them about? What had they done wrong?

Amanda leads them from the kitchen, through the dining room, and to the parlor in the front of the house. The two boys sit on a settee covered in a deep red, brocaded velvet. Neither has ever sat on something so fancy, and they perch themselves on the very edge.

Amanda returns from the kitchen carrying a tray

with glasses of milk, plates with large slices of pound cake, forks, and napkins. She sets everything on a coffee table in front of the settee. "Help yourselves," she says. "I'm going to go tell Miz Davis you're here."

Ansel and Willie look around the room. Sunlight streams through the lacy curtains and reflects off the glass-enclosed cases of books. Neither boy has ever seen so many books in one place.

"What do you think Miz Davis wants with us?" Ansel whispers to Willie.

"I don't know. We haven't done anything. Have we?"

"Not that I can remember."

Not knowing quite how to act, they remain balanced on the edge of the settee. They look hungrily at the milk and slices of cake, but they are afraid to touch either.

Esther Davis enters. She moves quickly, as if she has more energy than she can use in a day or a lifetime.

Even though Willie sees Miz Davis, both here and in the quarters, and Ansel sees her at church every Sunday and sometimes when she comes to the house to visit with his mother, neither boy can remember ever seeing her eyes on fire like they are now.

She sits down in an armchair facing the coffee table across from the boys on the settee. Amanda sits down in the companion armchair.

"Don't be shy," Esther says, smiling. Her voice is soft and deep. "You won't hurt that settee, and please, help yourselves to the milk and pound cake."

The boys relax, and placing napkins over their laps, they each take a plate and a fork and start eating the cake.

"Ansel? What do you want to be when you grow up?" Esther asks abruptly.

Ansel quickly swallows the morsel of cake he is chewing and wipes his mouth with the napkin. "Ma'am?"

"What do you want to be when you grow up?" Esther repeats.

Ansel looks at her, bewildered. He does not understand the question. He is going to work in the store with his father, and one day it will be his.

"Willie? What about you? What do you want to be when you grow up?"

Willie has been thinking about this for a long

time. He has never said it aloud, not even to his mother. But no one has ever asked him. Until now. He looks into Esther Davis's eyes.

"A doctor," he says simply.

"A doctor," his mother repeats, unable to believe what she is hearing. "Where did you get such an idea from?"

Willie looks at his mother. "Every time somebody in the quarters gets sick, and the white doctor don't come from town. I heard you say that Grandmamma wouldn't have died if the white doctor had come as soon as he was sent for."

Amanda's eyes get large, then fill with tears as she remembers what she believes was the unnecessary death of her mother. But she cries also because her son is dreaming, because in the time and place where they live, to dream is an act of courage.

Ansel did not know Willie wanted to be a doctor, did not know there was such a thing as a colored doctor.

Willie's saying he wants to be a doctor causes Ansel to remember the books he likes to read about a lawyer named Perry Mason. Ansel thought it might be fun to be a lawyer and solve murder mysteries.

"Ansel? What about you? Have you thought of what you might like to do when you grow up?"

He shrugs. "Maybe a lawyer. But Papa wouldn't let me. I'm supposed to take over the store."

"That's what your father wants. What do you want?"

Ansel shrugs again. "Never thought about it. My papa took over the store from his papa, and I'm supposed to take it over from my papa, and then my son will take it over from me."

"Is that the life you want for yourself?"

He doesn't like all these questions. No one has ever asked him what he wants. What was the point in wanting to do something if you couldn't? Seemed to him it was better not to want anything if your parents didn't want it, too.

Esther sees the look of bewilderment on the boys' faces as they turn their attention back to the milk and cake.

"If the two of you stay in this town, you will die but you won't know you're dead," she says with too much intensity. Her words come out as if she is angry with them when it is the town, the South, and life itself that make her furious.

But Willie and Ansel giggle.

"How can you be dead and not know it?" Willie asks. His question explains their giggles.

"Just look around!" Esther continues, even more animated. "Look at the people! There's not a dreamer among them. They are content with life in Davis as it is. Even your father, Ansel. I've known him all my life. I had high hopes for him. He has such a fine mind. He sat right here in this parlor, and we talked about going to school and never coming back to Davis. But his father convinced him there was nothing out there in the world, that everything he needed was right here in Davis. He was wrong, Ansel! Wrong!"

How could his father be wrong? Fathers were always right. Weren't they?

"What do *you* want for your life?" Esther continues insistently, desperately.

Ansel decides he does not like her. Who does she think she is to say his father is wrong? "What I want is not important. What Papa wants is what's important," he says flatly, stubbornly.

"Don't let your father do that to you!" Esther exclaims heatedly. "It's your life! Yours! Do you hear me? Yours!"

She is scaring them. She can see it in how their bodies have stiffened, in how they are looking at her, fear in their eyes, in how they have moved back to the edge of the settee like tiny birds about to take flight.

"Ma'am? We have to get back to the store. We have a lot of deliveries today."

Everyone knows Ansel is lying, and they are grateful for it.

Willie and Ansel get up, thank Esther and Amanda, and leave the house quickly.

4.

Each morning after Bert and Ansel leave for the store, Maureen stands in front of the oval mirror atop her dresser and stares. What she sees is a woman who is not as thin as she used to be, a woman whose body is becoming soft and round. Even her face is more fleshy. What has not changed are her eyes, which are so dark they seem to absorb light instead of reflect it.

For some moments she stands there. Repeatedly, she forces her lips up so that they curve at the ends. She parts her lips to reveal her teeth. That is what people do to make a smile, but she looks like she is grimacing in pain.

Because she can't smile, Bert stopped her from working in the store except on Saturdays.

Colored people don't seem to mind that her smile is filled with pain. They have an instinctive understanding of what it is to smile when you want to cry. They have to smile at any and every white person they see, no matter how young.

If they don't, somebody might complain to Cap'n Zeph that such-and-such a nigger has a sullen look on his face. A nigger who didn't smile was an uppity nigger, and there was no place this side of heaven for an uppity nigger.

But many of them looked forward to seeing Mister Bert's wife's face as much as whites looked forward to seeing Bert's.

It takes Maureen a while to understand why she looks forward to seeing the colored faces every Saturday. Their lips turn up at the ends and their lips part to reveal their teeth, but she sees only sadness in their eyes.

One Saturday morning she understands. Smiles begin in the eyes and flow downward to the lips.

Her eyes are dead.

She wonders: "When did I die?"

And that leads her to ask: "Was I ever really alive?"

"I breathe. My heart beats."

"But there is more to life than that. Isn't there?"

She has never been sure. When she was in high school, the girls talked about their boyfriends and what they did with them and when they were going to get married.

That must be like what it is to be alive, she had thought.

When Bert Anderson seemed interested in her, her spirit brightened.

She didn't know why Bert was interested in her. Her father didn't have a lot of money like his. Her father was a straw boss on Cap'n Zeph's plantation. That was only a little better than being colored.

Maureen had wanted to ask Bert what he saw in her. If he told her what that was, perhaps she could see it, too.

But she had been afraid to ask, afraid he would say he didn't see anything besides how big her breasts looked behind her starched blouses.

His eyes looked at them more than they did her face. But the other girls envied her when they realized she wasn't stuffing her bra with tissue like they were. They said she was lucky Bert was interested in her because he was a good catch.

Maureen thought her breasts must be bait.

The girls said she could let him do anything but never to go all the way. Not until they were married.

So she tolerated sitting in the backseat of his father's car, his hands groping at her blouse, one hand trying to unbutton it while the other tried to pry open her clenched knees.

She had thought his hands on her breasts would make her feel alive. But his hands were sweaty, and his slobbery kisses on her neck only made her feel wet with spit. What she had hated most of all was the wetness in her underpants, as if she had peed on herself, only she hadn't.

He had called her a tease, said she was torturing him, said if she loved him she would let him go all the way. But she couldn't.

What if she did and afterwards, he lost interest, having gotten what he wanted? That was what the girls at school said would happen if she let him.

One night he took her hand and placed it on his pants, against the hardness beneath. She didn't want her hand there, on that thing, and she took it away, but he grabbed it, put it back, and placed his on top and held it there, pressing with all his strength. She wanted to get out of the car, to go somewhere, anywhere, and die. He began to move his hardness against her captive hand, breathing faster and faster until he gave a small cry. His breathing slowed. The hardness beneath his pants went away like a balloon that all the air had come out of. He took his hand off hers. Her hand returned to her, but she did not want it.

One night, not long after this, it happened. Even now, even on this morning when she, a thirty-two-year-old woman, stared at herself in the mirror, she did not understand why, except she remembered thinking that maybe she would feel alive if she let him.

And so she did. And he did and it was over so quickly and all she had felt was pain. She remembered lying there in the backseat, glad she was wearing a dark skirt so the bloodstains would not show, wondering how she could get rid of her underpants without her mother knowing, and she was seized by a loneliness far deeper than the one she had lived in before that night.

Bert did not speak to her in school the next day. She saw him standing with some boys, a smirk on his face, and his friends turned to look at her as she walked by, and she knew that they knew, that everybody in school knew.

And when her period did not come, she knew.

She had thought her parents would be angry, but they seemed almost pleased. Her father, a crude and bitter man, said, "I'm glad you put them big titties of yours to good use." And her mother added, "You done good, girlie! The son of the second richest man in town is going to be your husband. You done good!"

They had not had a church wedding, nor had there been any guests, just her parents and his at the judge's office in the courthouse in Shireville.

Bert's parents were angry their son had let himself get trapped by a piece of white trash, which they told her to her face.

Bert said it was her fault, that she had led him on, that she had teased him so much that he had lost control and couldn't help himself.

She had not thought loneliness could get any more vast than it had been that night in the back of his car, but when the judge pronounced them "man and wife," and went on to say, "You may now kiss the bride," Bert had turned away from her, reached in his shirt pocket for a pack of cigarettes, took one out along with a book of matches, lit it, inhaled deeply, then, turning back toward her, slowly blew a stream of smoke in her face and walked out.

Her loneliness expanded until it devoured all possibilities of life.

Maureen blinked her eyes as if waking from a trance. She hurried downstairs and quickly washed and dried the breakfast dishes and utensils.

She had just finished when she heard a knock on the door. She hurried to the front of the house, opened the door, and Esther Davis came in.

Maureen looked at her. "You've been crying," she said flatly.

Esther nodded, and tears gushed from her eyes.

Of all the people Maureen had ever known, Esther was the only one who had always been kind to her. Maureen had been surprised to get a letter from Cambridge, Massachusetts.

Dear Maureen,

I know you are not what everyone is saying you are. You must be feeling very alone because no one understands. You are not alone, because I understand.

Your Friend,
Esther Davis

And so began a relationship through letters, letters that had gone back and forth from Davis to Cambridge, from Cambridge to Davis. When Esther moved back, the letters continued. Both women found that words flowed more freely from the nibs of pens than their tongues, though they were together on their weekly trips to the library in Shireville.

On this late morning the two women sit around the table in Maureen's kitchen. Each knows the other's most dreadful secrets; each knows the other's most poignant hopes. In their letters they have exchanged words limned with soul, words they could have never said face-to-face.

But on this day they sit across from each other. It is time. Esther stares down at the table; Maureen's eyes are fixed blankly on something behind Esther.

"I take it things didn't go well," Maureen says finally in her toneless voice.

Esther shakes her head slowly. "I don't know. I think I may have frightened them, especially Ansel."

"What did he say?"

"Not much. I think Willie is more of a dreamer than Ansel is. But Willie knows in the very marrow of his bones that there is no future here for him. Ansel can't see farther than someday taking over the store."

Maureen does not say anything for a while. She

had hoped this son of hers would not be the coward she is. From the moment she first felt him moving in her womb, she had been determined he would escape Davis. Perhaps he would get no further than a different loneliness in another place. That had to be better than the suffocating loneliness of Davis.

"Are you going to leave, anyway?" Maureen asks Esther.

Esther nods. "In September. I have to."

"I know."

"I feel guilty leaving you behind, leaving Amanda and Willie. I want to give them money enough so that they can go anywhere they want and get a new start. But Amanda says Big Willie will never leave here. This is the only place he has ever called home."

"I know how he feels. As much as I hate this place, I think I would hate being a stranger more."

"You're only a stranger the first day you're in a new place. The second day you already know more about the place than you did the day before."

Maureen smiles. "You would have made a good lawyer."

"Then I would have had to put my whole family in prison because I have never known a bigger bunch of crooks. Yet, I have a life of leisure, a life free of financial worry because of how much of a crook my grandfather and father were. I hate how they made their money, and yet, I am glad for the freedom it gives me."

Nothing more is said about Ansel.

When Esther leaves, Maureen knows she has only until September, which is not much time at all.

Inside her she senses a kernel of resolve forming. Though small, it gives her life a focus, a meaning, and as the corners of her mouth turn up, she feels a sparkle of light in her eyes.

5.

Late on the afternoon of the same day, Ansel and Willie are sitting behind the store. Each has a bottle of soda from which he drinks slowly, savoring its coldness against the heat of the day.

Finally Ansel speaks.

"What do you think about what Miz Esther said this morning?"

Although Ansel and Willie are the same age, Willie is as old as a cotton field. He knows his survival depends on how well he is able to perceive what a white person wants to hear and then says it before the white person knows that is what he or she wants to hear.

Until Ansel had almost called him that word this morning, he had just about forgotten that Ansel was white.

That could be dangerous. If he forgot that Ansel was, Ansel might remember that he was. And then what?

But his parents had assured him that Ansel and Mister Bert were not like a lot of other white people. They were more like Miz Davis than Cap'n Zeph. But

Willie isn't sure anymore.

"I didn't think nothing about what she said," Willie answers.

"You figure on staying in Davis the rest of your life?" Ansel wants to know.

"Where else I'm gon' go? And what would I do when I got there, if there was a there to get to."

Ansel ponders this for a minute. "I don't think I knew there was a there until Miz Esther said I didn't have to take over the store." He stops and gazes into the distance as if he is seeing something for the first time.

"I don't have to do what my papa does if I don't want to. I had never thought about that before this morning. I don't even have to stay here in Davis."

"Good for you," Willie says. There is resentment in his voice.

"Good for me what?"

"Good for you that you don't have to do what anybody says. Good for you that you can go somewhere else." Willie does not disguise the contempt he now feels for Ansel.

Ansel opens his mouth to say something, then closes it slowly. He looks at Willie, and he is ashamed.

He had forgotten what Willie cannot forget.

It is only at this moment that he understands the difference in their lives, the difference between one who could imagine that his life could be different, and one who knew that his life would not be, regardless of how much he dreamed.

Ansel wants to apologize, wants to say something that will take away the look of resentment on Willie's face, wants to say something that will take back what he almost called him that morning. But when he speaks, he is surprised at the words that come out, surprised at how fervently they come out.

"We've got to start dreaming, Willie. We've just got to!"

This is the last thing Willie expected Ansel to say. His use of "we" startles Willie. He resents Ansel for thinking that he is in the same position as Willie, but when he looks at Ansel, when he sees the look of anguish on his face, he remembers something his father told him, something that didn't make sense until now.

"Don't never let yourself be angry with white folks. Us niggers, we know things are in a bad way. But the white folks? They don't know that by keeping us down in a ditch, they got to be right here in the ditch with us. And because they don't know that, they worse off than we are."

Willie's face relaxes. He wants to dream; he wants to believe there is a there for him.

"How do we dream?" he wants to know.

He doesn't know that by asking the question, he has already begun.

Thursday Afternoon

Ansel likes to sit on a stool in the kitchen when his mother is cooking.

The worried, distracted look she wears like an old sweater that should have been thrown away a long time ago vanishes, and she becomes like a cup of hot chocolate on a cold morning.

He and his mother seldom talk when they are in the kitchen together. At such times it is as if all the questions have been asked and answered, so there is no need for either of them to speak.

But on this afternoon, the day after Esther Davis talked to him and Willie, a day when he went to work but early in the afternoon told his father he wasn't feeling well and came home, he needs to talk with his mother, needs to know if it is all right for him to dream.

"Do you ever think about living somewhere else?" he asks.

Maureen is slicing apples for the pie she is making. When she hears Ansel's question, her hands start trembling, but whether from fear or joy she does not know.

"Why do you ask?"

"Just asking," Ansel responds laconically, wishing his mother would tell him what she thinks for once rather than asking a question to answer his question.

"Yes," she says so quietly that he almost does not hear. "Yes, I do," she adds, a little more loudly.

Ansel's heart is beating so fast he is afraid it will run out of beats and stop. "Where would you live?"

"Oh, I don't know. Miss Esther thinks there's no place in the world like Cambridge up in Massachusetts."

"So why don't you go live there?"

"I wouldn't be any good in a place like that. Too big. Too many people. And what would I do? I don't know how to do anything except keep house and take care of my husband and my son."

Ansel is silent for a long time. He wants to ask her the most important question he will ever ask anyone, but what if she gives him the answer he does not want to hear? Or thinks he doesn't want to hear. What then?

Then it occurs to him. What if she says what he wants her to say?

That is even more frightening.

"Ma?"

She turns from the kitchen counter and looks at him for the first time. She hears a tremor in his voice. She knows what is coming.

"Do I have to take over the store when I grow up?"

There are moments in which one word can bestow life or abort it.

A mere word, one syllable from a parent to a child has the power of a commandment from God.

Maureen does not hesitate. "No."

Ansel does not have to wonder about her answer because her voice is loud and strong.

Her answer surprises him so much that he feels like he is trying to find his balance on the knife edge of the future she has just presented to him.

"Will Papa be mad if I don't?"

Maureen looks into the face of her son and sees

there the fear of and elation at a world of possibilities.

"Yes, but it's your life, Ansel. Being a failure at living your own life as best as you can is better than being a success living the life somebody else says you should live."

The silence returns. Maureen turns her attention back to the pie, which will turn out to be the best one she has ever made. Though mother and son do not move, they embrace each other in the silence that embraces them.

Friday

1.

It is evening. The sun has exited from the sky but forgotten to take the stifling heat of the day with it. On the unpaved, dusty streets, the heat settles into every corner and every crack of the houses.

In these days before air conditioners, the heat inside the houses is greater than that outside.

Everyone knows it will be at least midnight before it is cool enough to go to bed. So people sit on their porches, waiting with the patience that comes from knowing that it does no good to complain about what one cannot control.

Around the town square, white men sit on benches beneath the ancient oak tree.

Clouds are gathering in the southern sky, and

there are flashes of lightning and an occasional distant rumble of thunder. Even if the storm comes that way, and the old men around the square are sure it won't, it wouldn't necessarily cool things off. More often than not, a rain in August didn't do much good for the crops and only made the air hotter.

Bert and Ansel are closing the store. Bert locks the door, and father and son start walking slowly to the car, which is parked off the square, next to the church cemetery.

"Thanks for helping me fill out the orders," Bert says. "I started learning things like that from my papa when I was around your age. Before I know it, you'll be ready to take over from me."

Ansel does not know what to say. He liked helping his father, but when he tries to imagine working in the store for the rest of his life, he can't.

If only he knew what he wanted. Until he does, he doesn't see any point in saying anything to his father.

As father and son cross the street to the car, they see Big Willie hurrying out the front door of the church. He looks quickly to his right and left, and seeing Bert and Ansel, he runs to them.

"Mistah Bert, suh! I'm glad it's you. Yes, suh!" Willie is a tall and rather ungainly young man. His face looks as if it absorbed every death he witnessed, those he was agent of and those he was not. He is wearing a khaki military shirt with a private's stripe on the sleeve. But the shirt is dirty and torn, as if he has not taken it off since his discharge.

"Wasn't me, Mistah Bert. No, suh! I didn't have nothing to do with it, but I know I'm gon' get blamed for it. Something like this happen, nigger gets blamed every time. Yes, suh. Sho' do. But I ain't done it."

"What are you talking about, Willie?"

Willie points toward the church. "I seen him. I seen him just as sho' as I'm seeing you and Mistah Ansel. Yes, suh. The young Mistah Zeph."

Bert hurries to the church and goes inside. In the dim light at the front, he sees and does not want to believe what he sees.

"Ansel! Go outside!"

Instead of doing what his father tells him, Ansel says, "Papa? What's he doing?"

Zeph Davis the Third turns at the sounds of the voices. In his right hand is a knife. It is slick with

71

blood. On the floor in front of the altar lies a body, the skirt raised to reveal her nakedness.

Ansel does not wait for an answer from his father, who is still trying to understand what he is seeing. Ansel screams, "Mary Susan! Mary Susan!" and runs to the front of the church. He stops and stares at her nakedness. Then, realizing what he is doing, he pulls down the skirt to cover her.

In doing so, he sees a ripped blouse and severed bra. The exposed breasts are red and slick with blood.

He wants to stare, but feels that he shouldn't, that Mary Susan would not want him to.

He takes the blood-soaked blouse and pulls both sides over her bared breasts, careful not to touch them.

Zeph looks rapidly from Ansel to Bert, back and forth, back and forth, breathing heavily, not knowing what to do, what to say.

Then he sees Big Willie in the shadows at the back of the church.

"He did it!" Zeph shouts, pointing at Big Willie. "He did it!"

"Mistah Bert? Suh, look at me. Ain't no blood

nowhere on me. Look at him. He covered with blood, her blood."

"You know niggers, Bert!" Zeph breaks in. "They do all kinds of stuff with roots. That nigger probably got a mojo that can take blood off his hands."

"I seen him, Mistah Bert. I seen him. I was up in the balcony. I likes to sit up there when no one's around. It's real peaceful.

"That's where I was when the preacher's girl, Miz Mary, come in. I wanted to leave right then 'cause I knowed it wouldn't look good if I was alone in the same place with a white woman. But wasn't no way I could get out without her hearing. Seein' me, she might get the wrong idea and start screaming. So I just stayed right still.

"She went to the altar and knelt down to pray. I wondered what could be weighing so heavy on the heart of someone as young as she was. If she'd been a nigger gal, I could understand. Us niggers need all the prayer we can get. Yes, suh.

"Miz Mary hadn't been there long when I heard the door of the church open and he come in. I thought maybe the two of them had decided to meet up together at the church, but when she turned around to see who it was had come in and seen it was him, she say, 'What do you want? You get on outta here and leave me alone. I'm praying.'

"He don't pay no mind to what she say. He go up to her and grab her and try to kiss her. She push him away. She say, 'Get away from me or I'll kick you so hard you won't be able to move for a month.'

"That's when he whipped out his knife and before she could do anything, he was on her, stabbing her over and over. Then I seen him raise up her skirt, and I didn't want to see no more. Mistah Zeph was so caught up in what he was doing that he didn't see me, and I hurried out and that's when I seen you and your boy. That's the God's truth, Mistah Bert. You believe me, don't you? You'll tell the white folks it wasn't me. Won't you, Mistah Bert?"

"Who you going to believe, Bert? A nigger or a white man?"

Zeph notices that Bert is hesitating, that Bert is thinking about what the right thing to do is, and Zeph drops the knife on the floor next to Mary Susan's body, runs up the aisle and out of the church.

"Rape! Rape! Pastor's daughter been raped by a nigger!" Zeph is running and yelling at the same time. Over and over he shouts and the only words that are clear are "rape" and "nigger."

The men sitting on benches around the square, who, a mere instant before had not wanted to move against the heat, spring up and hurry to meet Zeph.

"That crazy, shell-shocked nigger who works around the church done raped and killed the preacher's daughter!" Zeph tells his eager listeners.

The men see the blood on his shirt, the blood on his hands, and they know. They know Zeph Davis. They had seen him just the other day walking toward the back of Anderson's store with the preacher's girl, and they had seen him come back by himself, and a little later, seen her come out. They know what didn't happen then, and they know what happened this evening. But they tell themselves Zeph got covered with blood because he was trying to save the pastor's daughter from that crazy nigger. Yes, that's how it was.

Some of the men hurry off into the night to spread the news to all those sitting on their porches. Soon people are rushing to the church, some walking, some running, some in cars. They get there in time to hear a loud scream, and rush inside to see Polly,

Reverend Dennis's wife, lying across the body of her only child.

Reverend Dennis hovers behind his wife and takes her gently by the shoulders, pulls her away from the body, and enfolds her in his arms.

Big Willie still stands at the back of the church, tears flowing down his face. He wants to run, but that would be like saying he did it.

But Mistah Bert knows the truth, him and the boy. They know the truth of the matter. Everything's gon' be all right.

Zeph rushes back into the church, a crowd following him. He sees Willie. "There the nigger is! Grab him!"

"Well, I be damned," someone says. "This is one brazen nigger! Instead of running, he stays around to admire what he done to a white girl!"

Big Willie is seized by several men, their eyes lust-blind with violence.

Willie's eyes plead with Bert Anderson. When those blue eyes turn quickly away from Willie's, he calls out, "Mistah Bert, suh. Please tell these gentlemen I had nothing to do with what happened to that girl. You know that's the God's truth, suh. Please tell 'em!"

Suddenly, everyone stops. All eyes are now on Bert.

Ansel had left Mary Susan's side when her parents came in. Now he stands next to his father, looking up at him, waiting for him to tell everyone who did it, who killed Mary Susan, his Mary Susan.

Bert does not have a smile for this occasion. His head turns toward Big Willie, but his eyes are looking past him, but are not focused on anyone or anything. Sweat glistens on his forehead and above his upper lip.

"What about it, Bert? Is that nigger telling the truth?"

Bert recognizes Zeph's voice. "Well, Willie claims Zeph done this," he says in a hoarse voice, as if he has swallowed his tears. "But—but no white man would do that to a white girl just entering the flower of southern womanhood."

Though Bert spoke so softly that only those next to him could hear, the crowd does not need to hear his words. They know what Bert had to say if he was going to continue living in Davis.

"Anybody gon' over to Shireville to get the sheriff?" someone asks.

"He's gon' fishing with his brother-in-law."

"Shouldn't we wait for him?"

"For what? We know who done it, and we know what needs to be done."

"And the sheriff would be mighty angry if we brought him back from his fishing trip to deal with a nigger."

"That's the God's truth!"

And the crowd moves Willie toward the square, toward the large oak tree.

Ansel does not understand. "Big Willie didn't do it, Papa," he says to his father in a quiet voice, mindful of Reverend and Mrs. Dennis at the front of the church, looking down at their daughter's body.

"Well, we don't actually know that," Bert responds to his son.

"Yes, we do," Ansel insists. "That's Zeph's knife. Everybody knows that's his knife. And Zeph is all bloody."

"This is grown-ups' business," Bert responds, angry now. "You hear me? We didn't see a damn thing. You understand me?"

Just then Reverend Dennis walks up.

"Bert? I believe the boys could probably use some of that good stout rope from your store. My daughter would be alive if I hadn't let you talk me into hiring that nigger. We all knew he was crazy. What in God's name were you thinking wanting that nigger to work here where he could do what he did to my daughter?"

"Reverend, I—"

"The boys could use some rope, Bert."

"Yes, Reverend. Let's go, Ansel."

"Get the rope by yourself!" Ansel says.

Bert grabs Ansel's upper arm and squeezes it tightly as he hurries him outside. "You listen to me," his voice quiet but hard. "I don't like this any more than you do. Don't you think I know it's wrong? Well, I do, but what I think is right and wrong is different from what they say is right and wrong. And at this moment, what I think is right and wrong ain't worth pig slop. You're going to come with me to get the rope, and we're going to stay around and watch whatever happens, whether we want to or not."

2.

When Bert and Ansel return to the square with the rope, a large bonfire is blazing beneath the tree. The crowd has swelled in size, and it looks like everybody in town is there. Though the fire only intensifies the stultifying heat of the night, the fire also makes it easy to see, and everyone's eyes are on Big Willie.

Two men hold him tightly by the arms while another ties his hands behind his back. Willie is bare chested because someone has ripped off his khaki shirt with its military stripe. His face is bloody, and blood pours from his mouth because anyone who wants to hit him does, using an ax handle someone took from Anderson's Store because everybody knows you'll break your hand if you hit a nigger's hard head with your fist.

Willie would have been beaten into unconsciousness if someone hadn't realized it would be better to keep him conscious so he would know, so he would feel what was happening to him.

Ansel looks around for his mother but doesn't see her. He didn't expect to. He sees her parents, though, his grandparents. He scarcely knows them because his mother does not let him visit them nor invite them to the house. They have big grins on their faces.

Everybody else's parents and grandparents are there, because he sees every kid from school. There are always bonfires under that tree every November before the homecoming football game, and this almost feels like that. Only thing missing are the cheerleaders, but they are there, just not in uniforms.

He sees the choir director from church, all the choir members, the Junior Choir, and the ushers.

Ansel's eyes wander away from the crowd to the road leading into Davis. He is not sure, but way up the street he thinks he sees Miz Davis, Little Willie, and Little Willie's mother standing next to a car.

Now that death is at hand, Big Willie is surprised that all the confusion that ordinarily occupies his mind has disappeared. He does not want to die, and yet, considering his life, he hopes death will free him from the evil he witnessed, the evil that robbed him of his mind, the evil that will soon take his life.

The people staring at Willie are uneasy because he is not begging them for his life, not crying tears of remorse, not acting like a nigger is supposed to act who raped a white girl, the pastor's daughter.

"You proud of what you did, nigger?" someone calls out.

"I ain't done nothing," Willie yells back. His voice has never been stronger, his words never more clear. "It was young Mistah Zeph done this. And y'all know it."

The crowd is hushed, not knowing how to react to a nigger who dares accuse a white man. Yet all eyes shift to where Zeph the Third stands next to his father. Cap'n Davis is not tall like his son, but short and thin. Perhaps it is his unprepossessing physique he compensates for by a remorseless attachment to power, a compulsive need to dominate the life of every man, woman, and child in the town that bears his surname.

He knows what his son has done. He does not disapprove. No one could be allowed to stand in the way of anything a Davis wanted, not even if it was the pastor's daughter. But the next day he will take his son to New Orleans or maybe Memphis. Cap'n Davis has uncles in both places with whom Zeph the Third could stay for a year or so.

Bert taps Ansel on the shoulder. "I'm going to open up the store," he whispers. "Hot night like this, that bonfire making things hotter, people are thirsty. Come on!"

Bert then turns to the man next to him. "Spread the word through the crowd. I'm going to open the store. I figure folks might appreciate a cold bottle of soda pop."

The man grins. "I'll tell folks. Save a root beer for me."

It could be the annual Fourth of July picnic. Not only were people drinking sodas, Cap'n Davis had brought some cases of moonshine whiskey into town, and Zeph the Third was selling them from the back of the truck. The only thing missing was a pig roasting, but a nigger would do.

Little children ride on the shoulders of their fathers so they can see better. Men stand with their arms around the waists of their wives or girlfriends. Somehow, Fred Fuller, the photographer from Shireville, got the word, and he is there with his camera and plenty of film and flash bulbs.

Ansel sits in the darkness behind the store. From inside he hears loud voices and laughter. He knows he should be helping his father, but he does not move.

Whether he looks into the darkness toward the field and the creek behind, or whether he closes his eyes, all he can see is Mary Susan's body. All he can hear is her voice calling out to him that she was sorry. She wanted to apologize, to make up, and he wouldn't let her.

If he had, maybe she would have been at the store with him instead of at church. He knew she had gone there to ask God to turn his heart away from anger and spite.

Ansel's entire body feels like it is in flames, and the flames will never die because the fuel on which they feed—sorrow and regret—will never be exhausted.

From outside there comes loud cheering. People in the store rush out.

"My papa told me about a lynching he went to once. Said wasn't nothing quite like it. I wish he were here 'cause I wonder if this one is better than the one he went to."

"My grandpappy told me that once every few years you had to lynch a nigger, whether one had done something or not. He said there was nothing like a lynching to keep niggers in their place, and nothing like a lynching to remind a white man who he is."

"I was a little girl when my parents took me to one. It wasn't in our town. We had to take the train to get there. That was my first time on a train. That train was full of folks going to the lynching. There'd been an article in the paper that said there was a nigger who'd raped a white woman and he was going to be lynched. A daytime lynching is better 'cause you can see more. We had so much fun that day. Somewhere at home I still have the picture of me on my daddy's shoulders looking at the nigger. Oh, I almost forgot! How could I forget that! They hung two niggers that day! You know what else happened that day. I met my Sammy. He was nine and I was seven, and we both knew we was going to marry each other. Eight years later we did. Just think. If not for that lynching, I never would have met him."

"Come on, Ansel. You can't hide back here. Folks will think we're nigger lovers if they don't see us out there by the tree."

"I don't care what they think."

"If you're going to be a successful storekeeper, you better start caring what they think. Those people are your bread and butter."

"I'm not going to be a storekeeper!"

The words come out of Ansel's mouth before he can stop them, but now that they are out, he's glad.

"You don't know what you're saying. We'll talk about this later."

Big Willie stands on a tower of wooden crates, the thick noose around his neck, the other end tied to a thick limb of the oak tree. Willie feels so calm, he is almost happy. He looks at the faces in a semicircle before him. No one will meet his eyes.

Reverend Dennis steps out of the crowd. "Let us bow our heads in prayer."

There is silence.

"Our Heavenly Father, we stand here tonight to make right a terrible wrong. You are a God of justice who has taught us right from wrong. Although hanging this nigger will not bring back my daughter, it will remove from our midst the one who, in his mad nigger lust, took her from us. We know, Heavenly Father, that you have already prepared his place in the hottest part of hell, where he will burn for eternity. In Jesus' name we pray. Amen."

"Amen," the crowd responds.

As the Reverend walks back into the crowd, people eagerly step forward to shake his hand, pat him on the back, express their condolences over his loss. Many of them will think back on this night when, the very next summer, the Reverend is caught with one of the girls from the Junior Choir, which is what had happened in Atlanta. The Reverend and his wife were barely given time to pack before they left Davis. No one knew where he went, and no one cared.

Reluctantly, Ansel follows his father out of the store, but he does not watch. He hears the wooden crates being kicked away, and the crowd's cheers.

When he finally opens his eyes, he sees the body of Big Willie hanging from a tree limb. His head is on his chest. The flames from the bonfire are licking at the soles of his feet. People stand in front of the body to have their pictures taken.

Eventually, the bonfire ebbs. As it does, a stillness slowly comes over the crowd. From somewhere there is a breeze. Big Willie's body sways slowly back and forth. The rope makes a squeaking sound as it rubs against the limb.

People start moving away. It is as if they have been in a stupor and only now are waking up to wonder where they are, and who did this awful thing. They know they didn't.

Then it starts to rain. The old-timers who always knew what the weather was going to be are surprised. They swore that the storm they saw in the southern sky would not come this far.

There are only a few drops at first, but suddenly it is as if the part of the sky where the rain is kept has broken, and the rain comes down so hard it hurts. People run to get away from the stinging drops.

Ansel and his father hurry back to the store to get out of the rain.

"Sold just about every bottle of pop we had," Bert says. "We're going to have to change the order. You want to do it?"

Ansel stands at the screen door, the rain spattering

on the sidewalk spraying him. He stares at the body of Big Willie, rain running down it like forgiveness.

Then he sees the white beam of car lights in the rain, and he watches as the car turns left at the end of the square and parks beneath the oak tree.

All four doors of the car open. Out of the driver's side steps Esther Davis. From the other door comes Little Willie's mother. Out of the back doors come three colored men and Little Willie.

He is the one who climbs the tree, crawls out onto the branch from which hangs the body of his father. Because the rope is thick and tightly woven, it takes him a few minutes before he is able to saw through it with a handsaw as the rain continues to come down.

When the body falls, the three men below catch it before it can fall into the sodden ashes of the bonfire.

Without thinking, Ansel runs out the door and toward the small group beneath the tree. The rain beats like fists against his head, his face, his body.

"Willie!" he shouts as loud as he can as lightning flashes back and forth across the sky and the sound of the thunder rattles the windows of every building in town.

"Willie!" he shouts again.

Little Willie turns. He knows whose voice is calling his name. He turns and looks at Ansel. Ansel does not know what he wanted to say, does not know what he wanted to do, but through the darkness he thinks he can see Little Willie's eyes staring at him and those eyes are filled with a hatred that began with the first African who walked off a slave ship, a hatred that would extend farther into the future than either boy could see. And seeing that hatred, Ansel realizes that he wanted to ask Little Willie to forgive him, to absolve him of responsibility, and that Little Willie would not, could not, should not.

As the body of Big Willie is placed gently inside the trunk of Miss Davis's car, his son who, from that night on, would never permit anyone to call him Little Willie or even Willie ever again, turns away from Ansel and hurries to the car.

Ansel watches as they drive into the night, back to the quarters.

As suddenly as it started, the rain stops. In the distance there is a faint, lingering rumble of thunder, and closer, the whine of mosquitoes.

Ansel walks slowly back toward the store where

his father stands, having witnessed the scene.

"Let's go home," Bert says quietly. "Someday you'll understand."

Ansel looks at his father. "Do you mean I'll understand why you let Big Willie die?"

When his father does not answer, Ansel walks away.

Friday Night, Later

The Anderson house is too far away from the center of town for Maureen to hear what is going on. Her parents stopped by to see if she wanted to "see a nigger get lynched."

Of course they knew she didn't, but why pass up an opportunity to show their resentment of her for not sharing some of that money they knew she and her husband had.

After they sped away, the tires of their car sending a thick cloud of dust onto the porch where she was sitting, she wished she had gone with them to get Ansel. She could have gotten a ride with one of her neighbors, all of whom had gone as if it was carnival time.

Where is Ansel? Why hasn't Bert taken him away from there, brought him home? she wonders.

Maureen waits, never moving from the porch. It is almost eleven when a car drives slowly down the road past her house. Then another and another. Lights go on in her neighbors' houses.

The storm that she has watched move slowly in the direction of Davis breaks, and the rain comes down like vengeance.

She goes inside, sits in the living room, and waits.

It is almost midnight when she hears Bert's car.

Ansel comes in first. She does not have to ask. He refuses to look at her.

His eyes move desperately around the room as if searching for a place to hide. She goes to him, folds him into her arms, and his sobs sound like rasping crows.

When Bert comes in, he doesn't want to look at her, either.

"How could you, Bert?" she asks softly. "How could you?"

"How could I what?"

"Couldn't you at least have brought Ansel home? He didn't need to be there."

"Yes, he did. He's going to be running the store one of these days. He had to be there. Folks would have talked if he hadn't been."

"Let 'em talk!" Ansel turns around and screams at his father. "Who cares what they say?"

"You better start learning to care what other people think of you," Bert responds. "A businessman has to get along with his customers, and sometimes that means doing things you aren't proud of."

"Like not telling the truth?" Ansel glares at his father.

Maureen looks from one to the other. "What happened? What's going on?"

"It was Zeph!" Ansel shouts. "Zeph killed Mary Susan. We were there. We saw him. We knew Willie's papa didn't do it."

Bert sighs. He looks at Maureen, a plea on his face. "What was I supposed to do? We would be on the way out of town right now if I had said it was Zeph. Do you think people would have believed me? They know I helped Big Willie get the job at the church. Damn Esther Davis! They know I've had Little Willie working at the store. All they would've said was that I'm a nigger lover, and they might have hung me, too. Reverend Dennis told me to my face that it was my fault his daughter was dead, that I should have known better than talk him into hiring Willie."

"Oh, dear God," Maureen says, tears coming into her eyes. "You mean to tell me you knew that poor man was innocent and you didn't do anything?"

"What do you think I could have done, Maureen? So what if he was innocent? So what if I know that Zeph is a mean, nasty son of a bitch? Do you think anybody in this town is going to do anything to anybody with the name Davis? Do you think any white man in this town would choose a nigger over a white man even if they knew the white man was guilty? What did you want me to do, Maureen?"

"Maybe it's not a matter of what I want you to do, but a matter of who you are, of who we are."

"No, it's a matter of living in peace with our neighbors and keeping a roof over our heads and food on the table."

"And you think that's more important than your son having a father he can look up to, a father he admires? You think that's more important than your son knowing his father is a liar and a coward?

"Go on, Bert. Do it. You've been wanting to do that since the day we got married and you blew cigarette smoke in my face rather than kiss me."

Bert lets his arm drop to his side.

There is a long and tense silence. It is as if each of them is holding his breath, that the next word, the next movement will decide the history of the world.

It is Maureen who speaks, and when she does her voice is quiet. "You don't have to be in Davis to put a roof over our heads and food on the table. So we would have had to leave town if you'd told the truth. So what? We could've gone some place and started again."

Bert shakes his head. "Go where? To some city up north? I'm a small-town country boy from the South. My grandparents are buried here, and so are my parents. And so will I. This is my home, Maureen. Everybody knows me here. If we moved someplace else, I'd be a nobody."

Maureen sighs and nods her head slowly. "I understand how you feel, Bert. Believe me. I do. Maybe it's too late for us, but I don't want Ansel to grow up in a town where people prefer to believe a lie and kill a man to prove the lie."

"What are you saying, Maureen?"

"I don't want my son to spend another minute in a town that would do what this town did tonight."

"What're you saying?" Bert asks again, sharply this time.

"Just telling you how I feel."

"I don't give a damn how you feel. You're not sending my boy away from here. I need him in the store; I need him to carry on the business."

"I don't give a damn what you need, Bert."

There is a stunned silence. Neither Bert nor Ansel has ever heard a swear word from Maureen's lips, and if they'd been asked, they would have said she didn't know any.

"What's gotten into you?" Bert asks softly. "This is not like you."

"How would you know what I'm like? When have you ever asked me a question about myself, about what I might have done on a given day, about the books I bring back from the library? When have you shown an interest in anything besides the store?"

Bert shakes his head. "I know what happened tonight was upsetting. You'll feel better in the morning. It's late and Ansel and I have to be at the store early tomorrow, well, it's today already."

"I'm not going to the store," Ansel tells his father. "I'm not going ever again. I hate that store. But don't forget to order more rope. All we had got used to hang Willie's papa."

Saturday Morning

1.

Bert and Maureen sit across from each other at the kitchen table. The only sounds are of his chewing the eggs, toast, and sausage she made for his breakfast, and the slurping noise as he drinks coffee.

Maureen is not eating. She seldom eats breakfast. She stares at him.

His eyes are fixed on his plate.

They have not spoken since their argument last night.

Bert is angry that his own family does not understand. All he is trying to do is provide for them. Why can't they understand that? He feels bad about what happened to Big Willie, but the nigger was half-crazy anyway. They just put him out of his misery.

Maureen knows she has reached a crossroads in her life. Until now her life has been as passive as a dead autumn leaf going wherever the wind pushes it.

This morning she feels more like the wind, active rather than passive. Is this what it is like to be alive? Is this pain of confusion and indecision life itself?

"It's Saturday," Bert says. "You not coming to the store today?"

"I don't think any colored people will be coming to town."

"You don't think I know that? But I bet everybody else will. I can't work the register and wait on people by myself. I need you and Ansel today."

Maureen has never said no to anyone. Not doing what someone wants you to is to risk losing their friendship, their love. But after last night she is not sure Bert was ever her friend, if he has ever loved her, or she him.

"I'm sure you'll manage," she says quietly.

"People are going to talk if they don't see you and Ansel in the store today. I can't have people thinking my family is a bunch of nigger lovers."

Maureen's eyes brighten. She smiles, though her lips do not part. "After what happened last night,

I think being a nigger lover is better than being white."

Bert angrily shoves his chair back from the table. "I don't know what in hell has got into you, woman, but you better get it out. You stay away from Esther Davis. She's the one been filling your head with foolish ideas. You wouldn't be saying these things to me if it wasn't for her. None of this would have happened if it wasn't for her. Just because she started you reading books, you acting like you're smarter than you are. Well, you're not, Maureen. You're still a dumb little piece of white trash who tricked me into marrying you. Stop trying to be something you ain't!"

Maureen has never seen him so angry. He does not draw back his hand as he did last night, but he does not have to. The hatred in his eyes hurts her far more than a blow to the face ever could.

"Have I made myself clear?" he shouts.

Maureen is trembling as she nods her head.

"Good. I've changed my mind about you and Ansel coming to the store today. Both your and his sympathy for that crazy nigger would be all over your faces like a billboard. And that wouldn't be good for business."

Maureen wants to ask him why what's good for business is more important than what's good for her, good for Ansel. Instead she says, meekly, "I'm sorry I'm not the person you'd like me to be."

"Just go back to being the simple girl I married. Everything will be fine then."

He leaves.

Maureen does not move from the table. She is not proud of herself for telling him what she thought he wanted to hear, for apologizing for who she is. But she had to find a way to put his anger and his hatred back in the cage where he had guarded them all these years.

But how long would they stay there? How long before the day comes when he cannot control them, and they break out of their cage, and his fist smashes into her face, again and again and again?

There is no longer a question of what to do. She has only to work out the how.

2.

Ansel has not slept.

Now it is morning. Already his bedroom at the top of the stairs is getting hotter.

He wants to go downstairs, but hears his father shouting. His stomach tightens. He looks frantically around his room for something, for anything he can use if it sounds like his father is hitting his mother.

When he hears the front door opening, then slamming shut, he hurries to the window to see his father getting in the car and driving away.

Ansel's stomach relaxes.

From downstairs he hears the phone ring. His mother picks up before the first ring is completed. He listens to her faint, muffled voice.

When he thinks she is off the phone, he goes downstairs.

His mother sits at the kitchen table.

She looks up at him standing in the doorway.

"Do you want some breakfast?" she asks, because that is what she does. She cooks meals, washes clothes, darns socks, sews on buttons that have come loose from pants and shirts.

Anybody could do those things. Anybody. But no one else can be his mother, and a mother is more than meals and laundry and sewing.

"I'm not hungry," Ansel says quietly.

"Neither am I," she responds.

Ansel looks at his father's dirty breakfast plate. What happened last night did not affect his appetite. That is all Ansel needs to know.

He sits down in a chair next to his mother.

She reaches out and takes his hand in hers. "I'm proud of you, Ansel."

"For what?" he wants to know. "I didn't do anything."

"You know what's right, which is more than I can say for your father."

"I hate him!"

"You mustn't say that, not even think it. He's your father. You can be angry with him, but you mustn't hate him."

"But what if he did something that was hateful? Is it all right to hate somebody who does hateful things?"

Maureen does not have an answer. Was it all right

104

for her to hate Bert because he had done something hateful when he married her?

The phone rings.

Maureen goes into the living room to answer it.

"I am so sorry, Reverend Dennis," she says. She was going to say something more, but she stops.

After a long pause she says, "I appreciate your call," and slowly puts the receiver back onto the cradle.

When she returns to her chair at the table, she is crying silently.

"What's the matter, Ma?"

She gets up, goes back to the living room, and returns with some facial tissue. She wipes her eyes and blows her nose. Then she looks at Ansel.

"That was Reverend Dennis. He said . . ." She stops. "He said he thought it best if we didn't come to church for a while, and that it would be better if we didn't come to Mary Susan's funeral."

"Why?" Ansel wants to know, tears coming to his eyes. "Why can't we go to the funeral?"

"He didn't say. All he said was it would be better if we didn't come."

"What did we do?"

"Maybe it's not a matter of what we did but who we are."

Yesterday at that time Ansel would not have understood her words. Yesterday at that time she would not have said them.

Monday Morning

The silence in the house has become hard.

Reverend Dennis had come in the store Saturday, come in the store when it was crowded, and said loudly, as if he was in the pulpit giving a sermon telling people to repent or suffer hellfire for eternity, that Bert was no longer welcome at the church, that Bert's family was not to attend Mary Susan's funeral, that he, Reverend Luther Dennis, blamed Bert for what happened because he had put a nigger where that nigger would be around a flower of southern womanhood, and everybody knew that no matter how hard a nigger tried, he couldn't stay away from a white girl.

There was a long embarrassed silence when the Reverend finished. Everybody knew the truth, and they blamed the Reverend's words on grief.

After the Reverend left the store, everybody there told Bert they didn't put any credence in what he'd said, that the Reverend didn't know what he was saying.

Even though the store experienced no drop-off in business, he took the Reverend's words seriously, and all of his anger at Reverend Dennis, at Zeph for what he had done, at Mary Susan for getting herself killed, at that dumb nigger for telling him the truth and believing that he could do something, at Esther Davis for meddling in his life, at Maureen for getting pregnant, and at Ansel for being born came to live in the house and now sat in every chair and atop each piece of furniture; it stood in every corner of every room. But it never spoke. It did not have to.

Anger *is* speech.

Maureen and Ansel leave a room when Bert enters; they eat after he has finished; they have whispered conversations when he is not in the room.

When he asks them what they were talking about, they say, "Nothing."

If it was nothing, why couldn't they say it where he could hear it?

On this particular morning, Maureen and Ansel sit at the breakfast table because Bert told them to. He eats his usual hearty breakfast.

Maureen had never noticed how much she hates him chewing with his mouth open. For almost fifteen years she has listened to him chewing his breakfast and dinner, and in all that time she has never told him what she says now.

"Can't you chew with your mouth closed? Why do you think anybody wants to listen to you eat?"

Bert glares at her, then chews all the louder, his mouth open wide so she can see the masticated food inside.

As soon as he leaves, Maureen hurries into the living room and dials a number on the phone. "He just left," she says.

When she returns to the kitchen, she looks at Ansel. "She's on her way."

Mother and son start to cry.

"I don't understand why you won't come?" Ansel says to her.

"I can't."

"But why?"

"I just can't. What's important is you're getting away from here. It's too late for me, but it's not too late for you."

They do not say anything else until Esther Davis drives up in her car.

Maureen and Ansel hug. Then she and Esther hug.

"Please come with us," Esther implores her. "You don't have to do what you're thinking about."

Maureen smiles, and Esther realizes it is the first genuine smile she has ever seen from Maureen.

"It's all right, Esther. It's all right. I'm not strong like you. I'm not very bright, either. And I'm certainly not pretty. All I ever had were big breasts. And now that I know Ansel is going to be all right, I feel at peace. I feel like I did one good thing with my life."

The two women hug again.

Having put his big suitcase in the back of the car where Big Willie's body had been, Ansel waits in the car.

As the car starts to move away, he turns to look at his mother. She is looking at him. He waves. She waves back.

He knows he will never see her again.

Epilogue

When I came downstairs that Saturday morning, I was no longer a child. I had seen two people murdered in one evening, people who occupied places in my heart. I understood that life could be extraordinarily cruel, that life was intrinsically unfair, and that there was no justice.

That morning I also understood Esther Davis's words about how a person could be alive and yet dead. I had only to think of my father.

When my mother asked me if I wanted to go to Massachusetts with Mama Esther, as I came to call her, I did not hesitate. Yes, I told her. Yes.

When we drove away that day, I knew I would not see my mother again. When Mama Esther and I arrived at her house in Cambridge, she handed me an envelope, a letter from my mother.

Dear Ansel,

When you read this, I will no longer be on this earth. Please do not be angry with me. I am not a brave person. I never knew if I had a purpose in life until I understood that I had to get you out of Davis, get you to somewhere you would be safe, to somewhere you could be the kind of person I know you are, the kind of person for whom there is no place in Davis. The events of the past few days spurred me to find what little courage I had. Now that courage is all used up. I know Esther will take good care of you.

Love,
Your Mother

Mama Esther knew my mother was planning to take a lot of sleeping pills, lie down on the bed in my room, and go to sleep. When my father came home that evening, I was gone and his wife was dead.

I have never blamed her for taking her life. It was only a matter of time before my father would have lost control of his anger. That evening in the living room when he drew back his arm, I saw murder in his eyes.

I did not go back for my mother's funeral.

My father did not ever get in touch, though everybody in Davis knew where I was and who I was with. But I did not get in touch with him, either. Yes, he was my father, but that did not give him a claim on my love, on my respect. Perhaps I could have loved him if I had respected him. I do not know if his telling the truth that night would have saved Willie. I doubt it. But by telling the truth, he would have saved his wife, his son, and himself.

I had finished Harvard, Harvard Law School, and was in my first year at a large firm in Boston when I received a letter from Zeph Davis the Third telling me that my father had died in a car accident. Zeph offered to buy the store from me since my father had not left a will. I knew the store was worth more than what Zeph offered, but I did not care.

I never saw Willie again. Mama Esther told me that they buried Big Willie the night he was lynched. That same night she drove Little Willie and his mother to Atlanta. Mama Esther heard from them almost every month. She shared their letters with me.

Never once did either Willie or his mother ask about me, and I knew Mama Esther had told them I was there with her.

She died a few weeks after my father. It was as if she waited until she knew I was established in the world, waited until Willie was a doctor. She had fulfilled her life's purpose.

I wrote and told Willie and his mother that she was dead. They never wrote back.

I wished Mama Esther had lived to meet my wife and my children. It would have been good if they could have known someone who knew me before. Perhaps she would have helped them understand that my silence is not a rejection of them but an inability to explain a time and a place where cruelty and hatred were as ordinary as bacon and eggs.

I've only gone back to Davis once. I had to attend a bar association meeting in Atlanta. After it was over, I rented a car and went to Davis.

When I drove into town, the Confederate soldier was still pointing up the street, except there was no rifle in his hands. I suppose it had worn out or been taken by some teenagers as a prank.

The stores on both sides of the street were empty.

I could make out a faded sign that read Anderson's General Store, except there was no store. When the interstate highway was built, there was no exit ramp at Davis. The town died. Everyone who was able moved away.

I saw Zeph sitting with some other white men on a bench under the oak tree. He was only two years my senior, but he looked thirty. Either the bib overalls he had on were too big, or he had lost a lot of weight. His hair was white, and gray stubbles of beard lined his face. He was dying of cancer, I learned later.

He saw me walking toward him and recognized me immediately. As I came near, I could smell the cheap moonshine whiskey on his breath.

I had not said a word, but he started yelling, saying he had given me a fair price for the store and if I thought I was going to get another dime out of him I was crazy.

Every other word was a swear word. I still had not said anything, but he acted as if I had. He wanted to know why I had come to town, and if I'd come back to try and pin the murder of the preacher's daughter on him, I was a blankity-blank liar 'cause everybody knowed that nigger ravished that girl and stabbed her to death. Nobody but a nigger would do something like that to a white girl. Everybody in town knew that.

As I turned to walk away, he pulled a knife from the pocket of his overalls. I tensed, but he took a brick of chewing tobacco from the same pocket. With his right thumb, he flicked the knife open and, as he cut off a plug of tobacco, I could see the knife plainly. It was the same one.

I went over to the church cemetery and found my mother's grave, my father's, and Mary Susan's. The stones at the head of each gave only the basic information—names and dates of birth and death. The cemetery itself was overgrown with weeds.

I wanted to find the grave of William Benton, for that was Big Willie's name. I drove out to what used to be the quarters. The only ones left were old. I found an old woman who remembered me and remembered Mama Esther. When I told her what I was looking for, she told me that his son had come a few years ago, had the body dug up and reburied in Atlanta.

I arranged to have the bodies of my mother and Mary Susan exhumed, put in new caskets, and shipped to Boston, where I had them reburied. They lie together now—Mama Esther, my mother, and Mary Susan.

I visit each week. I tell Mother and Mama Esther about my legal cases and the black kids I defend in court that the police have arrested for no reason other than because they are black.

I tell Mary Susan about the family she and I would have had. Each week I make up stories about "our children" to tell her.

Nothing I do eases the pain, not even putting everything on paper. I knew the truth that night, just as my father did. I kept quiet. And my being a child of fourteen is no excuse.

It was not that I could have saved Willie's father. But if I had said something, if I had told the truth, William Benton, Senior, would not have died alone. He would have had the solace of knowing that someone believed him, that someone was not afraid of the truth.

How do I atone for the sins of that time, of that place? I atone by forcing myself to remember the cruelties committed in the name of my race. By remembering, I hold the pain close to my heart. That was what William Benton, Senior, did by not forgetting the mountains of bodies.

Being guardians of those pains.

That is the least we can do for them—and ourselves.

Author's Note

I was born in 1939 and grew up in the Midwest and the South at a time when lynchings still occurred. They were not as frequent as they had been, but frequent enough to hang over my life and the lives of other young blacks as something that could happen to you if you did not "stay in your place."

I remember vividly the lynching of Emmett Till in Money, Mississippi, in 1955 and particularly the photographs in *Jet* magazine of his brutalized body. I also remember the lynching of Mack Charles Parker in 1959, also in Mississippi. When I did research in 1966 in Mississippi on black folklore and music, I interviewed people who, with no prompting from me, described lynchings they knew of. Lynching was a form of domestic terrorism designed to intimidate black people from seeking political and economic power as well as education. For the most part, it succeeded.

The word *lynching* comes from the name of a justice of the peace in Virginia in the late 1760s. Charles Lynch "and his neighbors created an informal court . . . to deal with suspected Tories and horse thieves." They were brought before Judge Lynch, found guilty, and "tied to a walnut tree in his front yard and given thirty-nine lashes." This extra-legal justice became known as Lynch's Law and, eventually, lynching.[1]

Lynching is the use of violence by a mob to circumvent the law and injure or kill a person accused of a crime. Between 1882 and 1968, approximately 4,743 men and women were lynched. Of that number, 70 percent—3,446—were black and 1,297 were white. These numbers represent only those lynchings for which there is a written record. There were lynchings that were never reported. Estimates of the number of lynchings before 1882 vary from 4,000 to 20,000, the number author Dorothy Sterling cites as the number killed by the white supremacist terror group, the Ku Klux Klan, between 1868 and 1871 alone. A Congressional investigation carried out in 1872 said that "as many as 2,000 blacks had been killed or wounded in Louisiana alone since the close of the Civil War."[2] Of the lower forty-eight states, only four states never had a lynching—Massachusetts, Connecticut, New Hampshire, and Rhode Island.

In most instances, lynchings were supported by state and local governments, the police, and the media. In 1899 a black man named Sam Hose was accused of murdering Alfred Cranford, a white landowner, and his baby, and raping the landowner's wife. The front page of the *Atlanta Constitution* had a headline that read, "Determined Mob After Hose; He Will Be Lynched if Caught." The subhead added, "Assailant of Mrs. Cranford May Be Brought to Palmetto and Burned at the Stake," Palmetto being a town in Georgia. Two trains of white people came from Atlanta to watch.

Lynchings were seen as social events. For one anticipated lynching in Memphis, Tennessee, in 1917, people camped out overnight at what was to be the site, and some parents sent "notes to school asking that their children be excused" so they could attend the lynching.[3] People posed for photographs in front of the hanging or burning body, and purchased "souvenirs," i.e., bones of the victim.

In the first decades of the twentieth century, the NAACP (National Association for the Advancement of Colored People) and other organizations publicized lynchings widely and tried to get the U.S. Congress to make lynching a federal crime, since the arrest and prosecution of lynchers was a rare occurrence. Indeed, the verdict of practically every lynching was that the person met his death "at the hands of persons unknown." To its shame, a federal law against lynching was not passed. In 2005 the United States Senate passed a resolution apologizing for never passing antilynching legislation. However, even in 2005, eight senators refused to sign the resolution.

The lynching described in this novel is not based on any particular one. And the lynching I describe here does not begin to describe the full horror of what actually occurred at lynchings. For those interested, I refer you to the books in the bibliography.

Having grown up with the prospect of being lynched as part of my awareness as a black child whose parents wanted me to reach adulthood, I have thought about lynchings often, from the point of view of what it was like to be lynched as well as what it was like to witness, to be a part of a lynching.

This may sound a little macabre, but as a writer, part of my responsibility is to wonder, "What was it like when . . . ?"

Several years ago a movie producer contacted me about the possibility of making a film based on my novel *The Autobiography of God*. Having been contacted several times in the past about making a movie from one of my books, I knew not to get excited because nothing had come from previous entreaties.

The producer called one evening to see if I would be interested in another idea. He had seen an article in the *New York Times* about an exhibit of postcards depicting lynchings of blacks. I knew of the exhibit and had the book, *Without Sanctuary: Lynching Photography in America* by James Allen.

As noted above and in this novel, photographers went to lynchings to take photographs of the victims as well as photographs of people posing next to the bodies of those lynched. These photographs were turned into postcards, purchased by those pictured at the lynching, and mailed to relatives and friends. James Allen, a white man from Georgia, spent twenty-five years searching for these postcards with their horrific images. (What does it say about America that such postcards had no problem being sent through the mail, but a postcard depicting a woman's breasts would have resulted in the arrest of the sender for using the mail for obscene material.)

The Hollywood producer wanted to know if I'd be interested in writing a film with lynching as the subject matter. I said yes, but that I wanted to write something from the point of view of a white boy. In looking at the postcards in *Without Sanctuary*, I had been struck by the number of them that showed children, boys and girls, present at lynchings. I remembered having had an exchange of letters in 1970 with George Woods, then children's book editor at the *New York Times*, about black children's books. Our letters were printed as an article in the Sunday *New York Times Book Review* on May 24, 1970. In my last one, I wrote: "White writers are so dishonest. Seldom have they written what they could have and should have, which is, the white side of racism. I'd like to see a children's novel about a little white boy who goes with his father to a lynching."

This notion had come to me reading Ralph Ginzburg's *100 Years of Lynching* when it was published in 1962. The book was a compilation of actual newspaper articles describing lynchings.

Over the course of my forty plus years as a writer, I have been struck, time and again, by how often I've had the germ of an idea for a book but have waited years, and sometimes decades, for that idea to gestate.

I wrote a seventy-five page treatment of the movie I envisioned about the white boy at a lynching. The producer read it, but his mind was set on a movie about a lynching from the perspective of blacks. There was no creative challenge for me in writing that story. I felt like it had been done, and I wasn't interested in writing something that would enable whites to shed crocodile tears for blacks.

The producer and I parted company amiably. Oddly I did not sit down immediately and begin work on this novel. I put the treatment in a folder and forgot about it.

I can't recall what happened, but five years later the treatment I had done came to mind. I read it over, sat down, and began this book.

It may seem odd for me to say that the book came very easily. But it did. It was as if the characters had been waiting for me, and characters I had not thought of presented themselves with their stories. Zeph Davis was a complete surprise, and the scene under the bridge in which he kills the frog came to me so easily that I was uncomfortable being in such proximity to my "inner sociopath."

While the subject matter is a lynching, on a deeper level, this is a novel about identity. Whom and what we identify ourselves with determines our characters, determines who we are, and what we do. Whose opinion matters to you the most? When you know that, when you know whom it is you most care about pleasing, you know who you are. We make choices every day that shape the content of our characters.

Lynchings can take many forms. The one described here is only more dramatic.

Unfortunately, the use of nooses as threats to blacks has become a cruel metaphor of our times. Over the past ten years, "about a dozen noose incidents a year came to the attention of civil rights groups," according to an op-ed article in the *New York Times* (November 25, 2007). That number escalated after an incident in Jena, Louisiana, where nooses were hung from a tree at the high school.

In 2007, there were between fifty and sixty noose

incidents—a black foreman at an ironworking plant in Pittsburgh found a hangman's noose at his work area; a black professor at Columbia University's Teachers College found a noose hanging from the doorknob of her office. Noose incidents were reported in Illinois, Minnesota, Indiana, Missouri, Louisiana, Texas, Pennsylvania, Alabama, Florida, New Jersey, North and South Carolina, Georgia, and Connecticut.

According to a 2005 Justice Department study, more than 190,000 hate crimes are reported every year. The Southern Poverty Law Center says the number of hate groups has risen by 40 percent, going from 602 groups in 2000 to 844 in 2006.

As much as many would like to believe that racism in America is on the wane, the truth is that in the hearts of some, it is, but in the hearts of all too many others, racism is not only not declining, it is acquiring new life.

Because of this country's history, a hangman's noose cannot be benign. It is a metaphor for a form of terrorism that touches every black life. Indeed, in 2008 an announcer on the Golf Channel was suspended for saying that young golfers who wanted to challenge Tiger Woods should "lynch him in a back alley."

Her comment was meant as a joke, but there is no humor to be found in lynching.

On February 11, 2008, at a ceremony commemorating African-American History Month, President George Bush said, "The noose is not a symbol of prairie justice, but of gross injustice. Displaying one is not a harmless prank. And 'lynching' is not a word to be mentioned in jest. As a civil society, we should be able to agree that noose displays and lynching jokes are deeply offensive. They are wrong. And they have no place in America today."

It is my conviction that the racial divides in the United States will not be overcome until lynchings of all kinds are as painful to nonblacks as they are to blacks, until each of us become guardians of the sufferings history has bequeathed us.

Julius Lester

[1] *At the Hands of Persons Unknown: The Lynching of Black America* by Philip Dray, Modern Library, New York, 2003, p. 21.

[2] *Ibid.*, p. 49.

[3] *Ibid.*, p. 232.

APPENDIX

It was surprising to me to learn that some whites were also lynched. Southerners used such lynchings as "evidence" that lynchings of blacks were not racially motivated, although whites were jailed for crimes that resulted in blacks being lynched. In addition, some lynchings of whites were directed at immigrants, such as the lynching of eleven Italians in New Orleans in 1891. Professor Heather Hartley, in her film, *Lynchings of Italians in America*, uncovered accounts of fifty lynchings of Italians in Louisiana, Mississippi, Florida, Colorado, Kentucky, Illinois, Washington, and New York between the years of 1885 and 1915. In addition, "Jewish and Chinese merchants, Mormon missionaries, and Catholic priests, Italian sugarcane workers and Hispanic cowhands all fell prey to lynch mobs." Lynchings of whites also occurred in the western states, giving some credence to the "necktie parties" of western movies.

—J.L.

Lynchings by State and Race, 1882–1968

STATE	WHITE	BLACK	TOTAL
Alabama	48	299	347
Arizona	31	0	31
Arkansas	58	226	284
California	41	2	43
Colorado	65	3	68
Delaware	0	1	1
Florida	25	257	282
Georgia	39	492	531
Idaho	20	0	20
Illinois	15	19	34
Indiana	33	14	47
Iowa	17	2	19
Kansas	35	19	54
Kentucky	63	142	205
Louisiana	56	335	391
Maine	1	0	1
Maryland	2	27	29
Michigan	7	1	8
Minnesota	5	4	9

STATE	WHITE	BLACK	TOTAL
Mississippi	42	539	581
Missouri	53	69	122
Montana	82	2	84
Nebraska	52	5	57
Nevada	6	0	6
New Jersey	1	1	2
New Mexico	33	3	36
New York	1	1	2
North Carolina	15	86	101
North Dakota	13	3	16
Ohio	10	16	26
Oklahoma	82	40	122
Oregon	20	1	21
Pennsylvania	2	6	8
South Carolina	4	156	160
South Dakota	27	0	27
Tennessee	47	204	251
Texas	141	352	493
Utah	6	2	8

STATE	WHITE	BLACK	TOTAL
Vermont	1	0	1
Virginia	17	83	100
Washington	25	1	26
West Virginia	20	28	48
Wisconsin	6	0	6
Wyoming	30	5	35
TOTAL	1297	3446	4743

Source: Archives, Tuskegee Institute
http://www.law.umkc.edu/faculty/projects/ftrials/shipp/lynchingsstate.html

BIBLIOGRAPHY

Brundage, W. Fitzhugh. *Lynching in the New South, Georgia and Virginia, 1880–1930*. Urbana and Chicago: University of Illinois Press, 1993.

Civil Rights Congress. *We Charge Genocide: The Crime of Government Against the Negro People*. New York: 1951.

Dray, Philip. *At the Hands of Persons Unknown: The Lynching of Black America*. New York: Modern Library, 2003.

Ginzburg, Ralph. *100 Years of Lynchings: A Shocking Documentary of Race Violence in America*. New York: Lancer Books, 1962.